The Blueprint

Van Cole

Published by Van Cole, 2023.

This is a work of fiction. Similarities to real people, places, or events are entirely coincidental.

THE BLUEPRINT

First edition. April 7, 2023.

Copyright © 2023 Van Cole.

ISBN: 979-8223421733

Written by Van Cole.

Table of Contents

The Blueprint
MM First Time Football Romance

By: Van Cole

Foreword

No one knows his secret.

Joey is the star quarterback for the Kites, a football teamed famed for its unstoppable winning streak these past five years. Everyone is counting on him to make the perfect pass – to take them to the championship.

So, they can't know he's gay.

In a very masculine and straight community, he would find nothing but ridicule. That's why he's kept quiet all these years, despite having the biggest crush on his best friend and agent.

Drew is the epitome of a man with his dark hair and ruggedly handsome good looks. Whenever he steps into the room, Joey can't help but hold his breath.

He's perfect.

Too perfect.

It'll never work.

Besides, Drew would never switch teams – sexually speaking. Every night he brings home a different girl, making it obvious that he's straight.

They don't stand a chance.

And yet, one night, after a drunken escapade, they end up naked in the same bed together.

Married.

The Winning Formula

Chapter 1

After a long day, there's nothing better than a nice, hot shower. Closing my eyes, I bit my bottom lip, enjoying the water washing over my body, melting away all the tension that had built up during practice. Slowly, I rolled my shoulders, wiggling my fingertips to relax my fatigued muscles.

Coach had put me through hell, forcing me to throw pass after pass until I thought my arm would fall off. I didn't even know why he was working me so hard. It was offseason. We were supposed to be taking things easy but instead, we just seemed to be straining ourselves more than ever.

Or, maybe, he was just picking on me. I might have been his star quarterback, the player who brought the team from ruins to riches, but still, it wasn't enough for him.

I sighed.

Don't get me wrong, I love football. It's been my passion for as long as I can remember but I never thought it would be this torturous. Then again, nothing good in life ever comes easy. If you want something, you have to work for it.

So, here I am.

On the bright side, today was the start of my vacation. Three whole weeks to myself. So far, I didn't have anything planned and I hoped to keep it that way. I needed the rest and relaxation.

About an hour later, I stepped out of the shower, bathroom filled with steam that fogged the mirrors. Reaching around blindly, I finally grabbed a towel off the rack, wrapping it around my waist.

Still dripping wet, I headed for the door. Before I could step over the threshold, the doorbell rang with a loud buzz.

My brows furrowed together in confusion.

Now, who could that be?

"One minute!" I called out, rushing toward my bedroom.

"Just open the door, Joey!" Came a familiar voice that made my heart stop inside my chest.

Drew.

I froze in the middle of the living room, staring at the door.

"I know you're in there."

"I'm... I'm not decent." I managed to answer despite the dryness of my lips. "Just give me a minute to get dressed."

"Do you have a towel on?"

"Yeah."

"Then, what's the big deal? Besides, it wouldn't be the first time I saw you naked."

His words made me blush crimson. He wasn't lying. As childhood best friends, there were plenty of times where we had been in the locker room together. Although, I was usually the one checking him out while he never even glanced my way.

I bit my lip, hesitating.

It was obvious that Drew and I played for different teams – sexually speaking. I had always been gay, keeping it secret throughout the years, feigning a lack of luck in finding the right girl. Drew, on the other hand, was a blatant lady's man. In college, he had brought home a new girl every weekend. It killed me to watch him flirting with these women, but I wasn't going to impose myself on a straight man, no matter how much I liked him.

"Joey! Come on! I really need to take a piss." He urged, banging on the door.

Knowing I couldn't keep him waiting, I stepped forward, unlocking the latch. I didn't even have the time to turn the doorknob when he came storming into my luxury apartment, making a b-line for the bathroom. He didn't even look my way.

Typical.

He never noticed me. At least, not in the way I wanted.

For a moment, I stood there, staring at the bathroom, imagining what he would look like naked, inside my shower. It was a fantasy I had thought about time and time again – a guilty pleasure. I knew it would never come to fruition, but it was still nice to think about. I had no doubt that Drew had the body of a God and a member to match.

On cue, my own member came to life between my legs. My blush deepened, spreading all over my face.

Quickly, I scurried into my bedroom, tossing on a pair of sweatpants and a plain t-shirt. I didn't plan to leave the apartment for the rest of the evening.

When I was done, I found Drew in the kitchen, looking into the fridge with a look of disappointment on his face.

"What's wrong?" I asked, tilting my head in question.

"What's wrong?" He repeated, looking at me. "What's wrong is that your fridge is empty. Seriously, how can you have a fridge but no beer?"

"You know I don't drink." I reminded him.

"Humph, you were never very fun on that front. But, you really need to live a little. A bit of alcohol isn't going to kill you."

"Oh yeah?" I crossed my arms over my chest. "So, if we both get trashed, who's going to drive us home? Or, did you forget that I'm always your designated driver?"

"Oh, don't use that as an excuse. If you wanted to drink, we could call a cab."

I rolled my eyes. "Why don't you drink some water, it might do you some good."

"Water? On a Friday night? Are you nuts?"

"You don't have any other options. I haven't gone grocery shopping."

He sighed. "I picked the wrong time to drop by, then."

"You always drop by." I pointed out, crossing the kitchen to grab a fresh apple off the table. As I took a bite, the juices dribbled down my chin.

To my surprise, Drew looked at me with an intense stare, dark eyes locked on my jaw. "You're making a mess." He finally said, shaking his head.

I shrugged, wiping my mouth, trying to look nonchalant. Still, I couldn't shake the tingling sensation that crept up my spine. There was something in that stare – something different – something new. What was it?

"Fine, where's the water?" He held up his hands in defeat. "I'm sure my liver will appreciate it or something."

With a chuckle, I tossed him a water bottle.

It slammed into his rock-hard chest, but he caught it with ease. "Nice catch."

"Nice throw." He said with a wink.

Oh, that infamous wink that had melted my heart long ago.

"Anyway, you know why I'm here, don't you? Or, did you forget?"

I tensed. I had a horrible memory, especially when it came to plans. "Um... I might have forgotten."

Drew shook his head. "I swear, you'd lose your head if it wasn't attached to your body."

I frowned. "Aw, come on, there's no reason to make me feel bad. What did I forget this time?"

"Just that we need to head to Vegas for Henry's bachelor's party."

I groaned. "Is that really this weekend?" I didn't particularly like Henry. He was one of the linebackers on our team and he was one mean son of a bitch. A few times, we had almost gotten into it. For the most part, I tried to keep my distance. The last thing I wanted to do was go to his bachelor's party. That sounded like a nightmare waiting to happen. "Do we really have to go?"

"Don't be such a sourpuss. He's having an open bar. We have to go."

"Again, I don't drink."

"You could start."

I rolled my eyes. "You're impossible, you know that."

"And yet, you've kept me around all these years."

"You act like I had a choice," I said, taking another bite of my apple.

"You could have signed up with another agent."

"Why would I do that when you're the best in your field?"

He smirked, a proud look on his face. "Damn right I am."

That was another thing I liked about Drew. He was confident. No matter what he did, he was always sure of himself. He never hesitated or doubted himself.

I wish I could say the same.

If I was anything like him, I would have come out of the closet by now but instead, I was living a lie, pretending to be a straight man when girls didn't attract me in the least.

It wasn't a life I liked to live but it was the one I had chosen.

"Plus, there will be a bunch of girls there. Maybe we can actually get you laid." He chuckled. "Seriously, man, when was the last time you got some?"

In that moment, I wanted to tell him the truth – the real reason why I had avoided every relationship with a woman.

I wanted him.

So, so bad.

Chapter 2

I don't remember the party, all I remember is waking up in a strange bed, in a strange room.

Where the hell was I?

When I tried to move, my head started to spin, temples throbbing. It felt as if someone had taken a sledgehammer to my head. I groaned, rolling over, trying to hide my face in a pillow but instead I was met with another man's hard, chiseled chest.

What the...?

I hesitated to open my eyes, too scared to face reality.

In those few agonizing seconds, I tried to piece together the night, but it was all one massive blur.

God.

I squeezed my eyes shut, trying to wake up from this weird nightmare but suddenly, a pair of strong arms wrapped around me, followed by someone nuzzling the top of my head. I tensed. Who was that? Ever so slowly, I dared to look up.

My heart stopped.

Drew!

In complete shock, I yanked myself away from him, falling clear off the bed. On my way down, I banged my head on the nightstand.

Bang!

"Ow!"

Drew sprang up, eyes wide open, a confused look on his face.

"What the fuck...?" He mumbled, glancing over the edge of the bed, spotting me sprawled on the floor, completely naked. "Joey? What the hell is going on? What are you doing in my bed? What are you doing in my room? Why the fuck are we both naked?"

I just stared at him, unable to answer. Honestly, I had no idea how we ended up in this situation. All I could think about was that we were just laying together in the same bed, completely naked. Did that mean...?

No, Drew would never do that with me...

Right...?

I rubbed my temples, wanting desperately to remember what had happened.

Drew got up and squatted beside me. "Are you alright?" He asked. "You banged your head pretty hard on the nightstand."

I was still in such a daze that I didn't quite register the pain throbbing through my skull. "Oh... yeah..." I said.

"You're bleeding." He frowned. "We should probably get you to a doctor. Coach would kill me if you went back with a concussion."

"I'm fine." I insisted. "It's just a little cut. I'll be okay." Slowly, I rose to my feet but as soon as I did so, the world started spinning. I stumbled forward, losing my balance. I felt my stomach churning and tightening in an act of queasiness.

I thought I was going to hit the floor for the second time when Drew caught me in his arms, cradling me against his chest. "I definitely need to take you to a doctor. You can't even stand up straight." He shook his head, gently guiding me onto the bed, sitting me down on the edge. "Stay here, I'm going to get the first aid kit."

Still completely naked, he padded through the hotel room to the adjoining bathroom.

I couldn't help but stare at his ass. It was perfect. Blush colored my face. How had we ended up in this situation? Why was he so okay with us both being naked? I know we have both seen each other in the locker room but this felt different. Very different. We were laying in the same bed doing God knows what together.

Desperately, I tried to search my foggy memory for answers, but I came up short. All I could really remember was having a few drinks and getting trashed.

It's like I say, nothing good ever comes from getting drunk.

So, why did I do it?

Before I could come up with an answer, Drew returned holding a small first aid kit. He was sporting a pair of sweatpants now that hung deliciously from his hip bones, exposing his oh so sexy V. I bit the inside of my lip, trying hard to keep my thoughts in check. The last thing I needed was a wild fantasy running through my head and causing me to have a massive boner in front of him. That wouldn't be awkward at all...

"Here." He handed me my pants.

"Right." I quickly put them on, glad that the nakedness was out of the picture. It was really becoming hard to focus.

When I was done, he carefully disinfected the cut on the back of my head. "I'd bandage it, but your hair is in the way. It's not actually that bad. It should be able to heal on its own." He said. "But, if you're feeling dizzy at all, then let me take you to the doctor."

"No... I think the dizziness is just all the drinking I did last night. Why did I let you convince me to come here?"

He looked at me for a moment. "Do you regret coming to Vegas with me?" There was a sudden seriousness in his voice that took me by surprise.

"No... that's not what I meant. I'm just saying that..." I stopped. Actually, I didn't even know what I was saying.

"Anyway, we should probably get going."

"Yeah." I agreed, getting up, trying to find my shirt. "Were we originally going to share a room together?" I was scared to ask the question, but it was burning a hole in my chest.

"No. But, this was the only room still available. Unfortunately, it only had one bed."

"Wait... do you know why we went to bed naked last night...?" I was blushing darker than ever, but I couldn't just leave all these questions unanswered.

"It was hot, I guess." He shrugged. "I don't actually remember all that much either. I drank you under the table." A smirk flashed across his face. "We were both plastered – that much I remember. After we left the bar... not so much. We probably got into trouble or something. There's probably a girl out there with my name tattooed on her ass, wondering where I am." He joked with a hearty chuckle.

A chill ran down my spine at his words. Right. Drew's still straight. Us sleeping together wouldn't change that. Of course not.

With a sense of disappointment weighing heavy on my shoulders, I looked down. When I did, my heart nearly stopped when I spotted it.

A ring.

A golden ring.

A wedding ring...

"Um... Drew..." I held up my hand to show him, too shocked to form the words.

His eyes widened as soon as he saw it. "What the fuck is that?"

"I don't know..."

He snatched my hand, inspecting it with a scrutinizing eye. Then, he looked down at his own hand. "Holy crap..." He whispered. "I have one too..."

I gulped.

Did this mean...?

We looked at each other and it was clear that we were both thinking the same thing.

We had gotten married... to each other.

He shook his head, running his fingers through his hair. "This can't be right." With an almost panicked expression on his face, he started to pace back and forth, making me anxious.

Was the idea of being married to me really so distressing? My heart tightened at the thought that Drew was disgusted by having me as a husband. Was it really that bad? I mean, I've been dreaming of marrying this man for years now.

"How did we get married?" He spat, turning to look at me. "Do you have any idea how this happened?"

I shook my head. "No..." I whispered, voice timid. I hated how upset he was by the idea. "Look, why don't we just take a deep breath and think this through. One of us is bound to remember if we just try hard enough."

"Right..." Drew continued to pace around the room.

I occupied myself by looking for my shirt.

"Wait!" He shouted abruptly.

I jolted in place. "What?"

"Turn around." He demanded, grabbing me by the shoulders and bending me over ever so slightly.

I blushed.

If this was a dream... things were about to get dirty real fast. But, instead, nothing happened.

Silence filled the room, making me nervous. "Drew? What's going on?"

"You have a fucking tattoo..."

"What are you talking about?" I asked. "You're kidding, right? You know I would never get a tattoo..."

"Well, it's right fucking there." He pointed even though I couldn't see.

"What... what is it?" I was scared to ask.

This morning was just turning into one chaotic nightmare. Maybe, if I waited long enough, I would wake up safe and sound in my bed but by the pounding of my heart, I could tell this was real. A horrifying reality.

"It's my name..."

"What?"

"It says 'Drew,' dammit." He growled. "How the fuck did this happen?"

I straightened up, turning to face him. "Hey, calm down. This isn't my fault. I don't even remember what happened."

"Neither do I! That's the problem..." He sighed. "I can't believe we are married... This can't be happening."

He really hated the idea of being with me.

Damn, that hurt.

Silently, I looked around the room for clues. There had to be a way to get to the bottom of this – to make all this right.

Finally, near the coffee machine, I found a folded-up piece of paper.

Our marriage license.

Well, now there was no doubt about it.

I was officially married to Drew Cohen.

I was Mr. Cohen now...

Chapter 3

Drew came up behind me and snatched the piece of paper out of my hand. Quickly, he scanned the text. "We have to go down to the chapel and see if we can't get this marriage annulled. Two straight dudes can't get married. It would ruin our dating game."

Right.

Two straight dudes.

In that moment, I wanted to tell him the truth, to finally tell him how I really felt, but I just couldn't bring myself to do it. He obviously hated the idea of being with me and I could never force him into a relationship like that. So, I would just have to suck it up for his sake.

Sigh.

***

It took us a while to find the chapel. It was tucked away inside a casino, behind a couple of playing tables. Drew eyed the table with suspicion. Whenever he was drunk, he liked to gamble. Not only that, he liked to make bets.

Maybe that's what this was. One big failed bet.

But it didn't even matter.

Drew didn't want to be my husband. I could dream all I wanted but it would never come true.

That's just how life works.

Sometimes you just don't get what you want.

"Come on... where's the receptionist?" Drew asked, growing impatient as we waited by the front desk. He still held onto the marriage license. "When we get back, we act like this never happened."

I nodded.

What other choice did I have?

Besides, if anyone found out I was gay, it would probably ruin my career in football. I'd be kicked out of the league in no time.

Finally, an older woman with wild hair and bright red heels walked up to the desk. She took her time, eventually plopping down in her chair before looking up at us with a bored expression on her face. "May I help you?"

"Yes. I don't know what happened last night but somehow, we got married. But, that's a mistake. We can't be married." He handed her the license. "This has to be some sort of misunderstanding."

She glanced at the piece of paper like someone who has seen this sort of scenario play out a hundred times before. "There's no mistake."

"There has to be. How can we be married?"

"We don't discriminate against any sexuality."

"I'm not gay!" Drew protested.

"Well, that's not what it looked like last night."

"Wait... you were here last night?" I asked, joining the conversation. Maybe she could help fill in some of the missing gaps in our memories.

"Mhm. I'm always here. My husband is the chaplain." She explained, looking at her nails. Without skipping a beat, she grabbed a file from her pencil holder and started to shape them right in front of us.

"Is he here?" I asked.

"Mhm. Right through those set of double doors." She pointed her pinky in their direction. "He shouldn't be busy. Probably asleep in the pews."

"Thanks." I nodded in appreciation, but she wasn't even looking at us anymore.

Drew had fallen silent, brows furrowed together. I knew that look. He was thinking – thinking hard.

"We'll find a way to get out of this," I whispered, trying to comfort him even though saying those words broke my heart.

Still, he said nothing.

So, I stepped forward, leading the way to the chaplain.

Inside, the ceremony room was actually quite nice. Well, as nice as a Vegas Chapel can be. Red carpet. Gold curtains hanging around the altar. Chandeliers hanging from the ceiling.

In the front, a man dressed in white vestments sat with his head slumped forward onto his chest.

As we got closer, I could hear his snoring.

Drew slowed down.

I glanced back at him. "Is everything alright?"

There was this glazed over look in his eyes.

"Drew?" I placed a hand on his shoulder trying to rouse him from his trance.

He blinked, looking at me like he was seeing me for the first time. "Sorry..." He mumbled. "Let's just talk to this man and get this over with."

I nodded.

We walked down the center aisle together. As we did, I couldn't help but reimagine what had happened last night. Did we walk hand in hand to the altar? Did we kiss after our 'I dos'? There was so much I wanted to know but the cloud of mystery was so thick that I doubted it would ever fade away.

Once we reached the chaplain, I shook him gently.

Abruptly, he woke up with a start, throwing his hands up, nearly hitting me in the face.

I managed to jump out of harm's way, bumping into Drew, practically toppling us over, but, somehow, he managed to keep us steady, arms naturally wrapping around my waist, pinning me tight against his body.

My heart skipped a beat.

It felt so good to be in his arms like that.

But, all too quickly, he let go of me.

We didn't make eye contact.

"Ah, I remember you two." The chaplain said with a smile. "Great couple. I could really see the love in your eyes."

Love?

I nearly choked at the sound of that word.

Yes, I had feelings for Drew. Strong feelings. But, I didn't know if I was ready to call it love...

He smiled, rising to his feet. "What can I do for you this fine morning?"

"We need to get the marriage annulled or whatever," Drew said, holding out the license. "There's some sort of misunderstanding. We can't be married. We're both straight..."

The chaplain chuckled. "You can't get the marriage annulled." He took the license from Drew and turned it over. "When you signed this, you agreed that you'd remain a couple for at least three months. From that point forward, you can apply for a divorce."

"A divorce?" I asked. The word felt dirty.

He nodded. "Although, I would not advise you to do that."

"Why not?" Drew growled.

"From what I saw last night, you two were made for each other."

"And, what exactly did you see last night?"

"A couple that really cared for each other." He said, looking Drew in the eye. "But, you are free to do as you like. It is your life, after all."

He sighed. "So, until the three months are over, we're stuck together."

"Yes."

"Great." He mumbled.

I just stood there feeling like shit. Of course, Drew would want nothing to do with me. He could get any girl in the world but now, he was stuck with me. He probably hated me.

With a sour expression on his face, he turned on his heels and headed out the door.

I quickly followed him.

Once we were back in the casino, he turned to look at me. "No one is to know about this. We keep it under wraps until we can get a divorce. Okay?"

"Okay," I answered, numbly. This was torturous. For years, all I wanted was a relationship with this man and now that I had it, I couldn't keep it. With a heavy heart, I watched Drew slip off his wedding ring and slip it into his pocket. I couldn't bring myself to do the same. I wanted to hold onto the fantasy just a little bit longer.

Eventually, we arrived at our hotel room. Instantly, Drew grabbed his phone, making phone call after phone call, asking 'hypothetical' questions, trying to figure out how to get a divorce as soon as possible.

Sigh.

He really disliked the idea of being married to me...

A part of me wished he would just give it a chance. Not much. Just a small sliver of hope that maybe, just maybe, things could work out between us. But, of course, that was asking too much. Drew was straight. He didn't find me attractive.

I was just a friend.

And all this was just a mistake to him.

In the middle of one of his calls, he suddenly threw his phone on the bed. "That was Jenkins. He's pissed. Apparently, he told Henry that he couldn't have his bachelor's party this weekend because you have practice this week."

"What? No, we don't." I said. "We have the next two weeks off."

"That's not what he told me."

"Well, he's wrong."

"Well, he's certainly pissed that his whole team is in Vegas getting trashed. And, that apparently, Henry got himself thrown in jail last night."

"Damn. Seems like we weren't the only ones with a wild night..."

He shot me a look. "We didn't have a wild night."

"Well, I didn't mean in bed or anything..." I blushed deeply. "I think we just fell asleep together. I wasn't implying that we... you know... we would never do that..." I started to ramble, growing nervous under the heat of his gaze. "I mean..."

He shook his head. "Never mind. Let's just try to pretend it never happened."

Right.

Easier said than done.

Especially when you've wanted this to happen for a while now. But, sure, I'll try to forget I'm married to my crush. Totally doable.

Before we could say anything else, there was a knock on the door.

We both froze, looking at each other.

"Who's that?" Drew mouthed.

"How should I know?"

"Did you order room service?"

I shook my head.

Slowly, Drew approached the door, looking through the peephole. "There's no one there..." He said, sounding confused.

Quickly, he unlocked the door, swinging it back.

By his feet was a loaded gift basket, painted in pink. It was very girlie.

"What the hell is this?"

"I don't know..." I glanced over his shoulder. "Maybe it's a mistake." Carefully, I turned over the tag.

For Mr. and Mr. Cohen.

"Um... Drew..." I tugged on the tag to get him to look at it.

He groaned. "Of course."

With no other choice, we brought it into the room, laying it on the bed.

"Should we open it?" I asked.

"Technically, it's ours, so yeah, I guess. We're already married, we might as well reap some of the benefits, even if it doesn't last."

The second I heard him say 'married' my heart sped up just a little bit faster only to be shattered to smithereens with his next breath. He was determined to nullify this marriage.

Why couldn't he just give it a chance?

Why couldn't he see how much I liked him?

But maybe I was asking too much of him... Or, I was a fool, trying to live out a dream.

Drew started to pull back the wrapping paper, exposing a plethora of expensive chocolates. With a shrug, he popped one into his mouth. "Do you want one?" He asked.

"Sure..." I grabbed one for myself, but it tasted bitter in my mouth.

"What's this?" He asked, fishing out an envelope from the bottom.

Congratulations!

The word was printed in a flowing golden script. I didn't have much time to look at it before Drew turned over the envelope and tore the seal, pulling out the card that was inside.

When he flipped it open, two tickets fell out.

My eyes widened.

Round trip flights to Jamaica?

"What does it say?" I asked, curiosity getting the best of me. This felt like a mistake.

"Dear Mr. and Mr. Cohen." He paused, practically cringing at those words. He wet his lips, starting again. "Dear Mr. and Mr. Cohen. We were happy to help you celebrate your love last night. As a sign of appreciation for using our services, we have entered you in a casino drawing. All couples that come through our chapel receive one entry into the contest. And, you have been chosen as the lucky winners! Please enjoy this all-expense-paid vacation to Jamaica for two. We hope you have an amazing time on your honeymoon!" He read slowly and clearly.

I looked up at him, not quite sure what to say.

A honeymoon? With Drew?

The thought excited me.

But I knew Drew didn't feel the same.

Two weeks alone with me would probably be torture for him.

He'd never want to go.

Chapter 4

We were silent for a long time, just staring at the tickets. Neither one of us knew how to react.

Should I say something?

A part of me wanted to but at the same time, it felt like my throat had closed, making it impossible to speak. Meanwhile, my mind was running wild, picturing a honeymoon with Drew. In a perfect world, it would be an amazing time filled with long days on the beach and even longer nights in bed. But, I knew all that was nothing more than a fantasy.

He would never agree to go with me.

Suddenly, a wave of dizziness washed over me. I blinked, trying to steady myself but the world kept spinning around and around. The edges of my vision grew blurry. I leaned forward, holding my stomach, doing everything I could to keep from getting sick.

It didn't work.

Doubling over, I threw up on the ground, retching up everything I had eaten in the last twelve hours. I was about to collapse onto the ground when I felt Drew holding onto me, holding my hair back.

I groaned in pain, head throbbing.

"We need to get you to a doctor." He said with a firm voice. I knew he wasn't going to let me convince him otherwise.

Slowly, he guided me to the bathroom, sitting me down on the soft bath mat, right next to the toilet in case my stomach decided to give me trouble again. "Wait here." He said, disappearing to find his phone.

I tilted my head back, pressing my cheek against the cool wall towel. I was so embarrassed. The last thing I wanted was for Drew to see me like this. I probably looked like a mess.

He definitely wasn't going to find me attractive now...

I sighed, hugging my knees to my chest, just trying to keep my breathing at a normal rhythm.

Had I really hit my head that hard on the nightstand?

Soon enough, Drew returned. "Are you okay to walk?"

"I... I think so..." I answered.

"Here, let me help you." He said, slinging my arm around his neck for support. "But, if you can't walk, I don't mind carrying you."

I blushed like fire. "No, no, you don't need to carry me. I should be fine."

He nodded. "Alright." Together, we left our hotel room and entered the elevator. There, the small space made me acutely aware of how close we were.

My heart was beating fast, maybe even loud enough for him to hear it.

There were so many things I wanted to do but I didn't have the courage to do any of them. Maybe, one little kiss would be enough to change his mind about me, but I'd never be able to bring myself to do it. He'd probably hate me for the rest of my life if I tried, anyway. So, I was forced to simply imagine the sweetness of those lips – a sweetness I would never taste.

Eventually, we reached the hotel parking garage. Drew very gently helped me into the passenger seat, handling me with the utmost care. The way he looked at me made my heart flutter. There was worry in his eyes.

"Just hold on, I'll get you to the hospital in no time." He said, rounding the car and jumping behind the wheel. "Let's just hope that you don't have a concussion, or your coach is going to kill me."

"It's probably just the hangover."

"Well, I hope so." To my surprise, he reached over, laying a hand on my thigh, squeezing gently. "I don't want you to get hurt."

I froze, looking down at his hand. It was dangerously close to my member.

He seemed to notice my tension because he looked over and quickly snapped his hand back onto the wheel. "Sorry." He said quickly. "I didn't mean to do that." A second later, he rubbed his palm against his pants, as if trying to get rid of our momentary contact.

Awkwardly, we rode in silence. I closed my eyes, arms folded over my chest, just trying to keep myself from getting sick. Every movement the car made churned my stomach. It felt like I was on a ship during a turbulent storm.

What was happening to me?

Alcohol never affected me this badly before...

But, then again, maybe it wasn't the alcohol doing all this.

No.

I can't have a concussion.

It could cost me the season...

"Are you okay?" Drew asked, finally breaking the thick silence that had settled around us. "You aren't going to get sick, are you? If you are, just let me know and I'll pull over."

"I'm okay," I said through gritted teeth, breathing through my nose. "I'm just a little queasy but I think I've thrown up everything I have to throw up."

"Oh... well, just hang in there. The hospital is just up ahead." He paused, adjusting his grip on the wheel. "I should have brought you to the hospital earlier. We could already have this sorted out. I'm sorry."

I turned to look at him. "It's not your fault."

He looked away, an almost guilty expression on his face.

A few minutes later, he pulled into the hospital's parking lot. Before I could get out, he was already opening the door for me, offering his hand.

Shyly, I placed my hand on his.

As soon as our skin touched, a current of electricity crawled underneath it, wrapping around my spine, and settling inside my heart. It was invigorating. I found myself breathless, just staring at him, pushing up against his car.

God, he was so close. His hips were nearly touching mine. And, he was looking at me with this intense stare that made me shiver.

He leaned forward, looking like he was about to kiss me.

My heart skipped a beat. I held my breath.

Was this the moment I had been waiting for?

Only, it never came.

He simply took my arm and wrapped it around his neck, supporting me into the emergency room. There, he took command of the situation, demanding a doctor.

The nurse gave him a nasty stare as she handed over a clipboard. "You have to fill out this paperwork and then we will be with you just as soon as we can."

"Is this really necessary?" Drew complained. He hated paperwork. I was usually the one that did it for him.

"Yes." She said, pursing her lips together.

He looked like he was about to argue with her, so I placed a hand on his shoulder, squeezing it ever so gently. "It's alright. We'll fill it out." I took the clipboard from him before heading for the waiting room.

"What are you doing?" He asked, sitting beside me.

I squinted at the page, trying to focus on the words but all the letters were blurred together, dancing around the page.

There was definitely something wrong with me.

With a sigh, he grabbed the clipboard. "Let me do it. You're obviously in no condition to do it yourself." He paused, looking me over with that same level of worry in his eyes.

It made me feel warm inside to know that he genuinely cared about me. I knew we were friends, but this almost seemed different. I can't quite explain it but the way he looked at me, it was like he was afraid to lose me.

"Why don't you rest a little too? This place is pretty packed. It might take some time for them to get to you and I don't think I can charm that nurse with my good looks."

I chuckled. "I don't know, you're pretty handsome." I nearly panicked the second the words had escaped my mouth. I don't know what I was thinking. I guess I wasn't thinking at all. I just kind of... said what was on my mind.

He looked down at me, tilting his head ever so slightly but he didn't bother to comment on it.

Great.

I'm such an idiot.

Quietly, he filled out my chart, knowing most of my information. Some questions he asked me personally, noting my answers on the page.

Then came the awkward one.

"Are you sexually active?"

My face turned into a legitimate tomato.

I didn't want to answer that question.

"Um..."

He raised an eyebrow in question but didn't say a word.

I gulped. Well, this is embarrassing. "No..."

"Alright." He checked off the box and moved on.

What?

That's it?

I expected him to make some sort of sly commented. But, instead, he just seemed to accept the fact as if he already knew it. Was it that obvious?

Damn.

When he was done, he returned the clipboard to the nurse who simply nodded her head and went back to playing some game on her phone. I could hear the occasional power-up whenever she made a particularly good move.

"This is ridiculous," Drew grumbled. "No wonder this place is packed. No one is working. That woman is doing nothing other than sitting on her ass."

"Drew... there's no need to be rude..." I glanced over at the nurse, hoping she couldn't hear what we were saying.

"I'm just upset that you need help and aren't getting it because some people don't want to do their jobs."

"I'm sure they're doing the best they can..." I said, trying to neutralize the situation. I could tell by the way Drew's jaw was clenched that he was getting angry.

"Like hell they are. You could die out here and they wouldn't even bat an eyelash."

"That's not true."

Drew shook his head and looked straight into my eyes. "You're just too nice, Joey. I love that about you, but that heart of gold is going to get you hurt one day. People are cruel. And, girls are the worst."

I bit the inside of my lip. He still thought I was straight. I mean, why would he think otherwise? He probably wouldn't be here with me if he knew I was gay and crushing on him.

"You should rest." He finally said, taking my head and gently laying it on his chest.

"What are you doing?"

"Trying to make you comfortable." He explained as if it were the most natural thing in the world.

"But..."

"Don't worry about it. We're married now, right? No one's going to care if we cuddle a little bit."

My blush was getting so bad that I thought it would burn right through my cheeks. I couldn't understand him at this point. On one hand, he seemed to hate the idea of being married to me, and then, on the other, he says things like that. Honestly, I didn't know what to make of it.

So, I simply rested my head on his chest, savoring the moment. I smiled when I heard the thump, thump, thump of his heartbeat. It was slow and steady. Soothing. I felt like I could listen to it all day long.

And, maybe, at the rate of service in this place, I would do just that.

***

I must have fallen asleep because the next thing I know, Drew is shaking me. I blinked, eyes bombarded with a bright white light.

"Ugh…"

"Shh, don't move too fast. The doctor's finally here to see you now." He explained. "But, take your time." Gently, he placed a hand on the small of my back to support me.

It sent a tingle right through my spine, making my knees weak. If I thought it was hard to walk before, it would be nearly impossible now.

But, somehow, we managed to shuffle into the exam room where a middle-aged doctor was waiting for us.

"Hello." He greeted with a flat voice. "I'm Doctor Campbell." He held out his hand.

Drew took it in a firm shake first before I followed suit. His hand was cold – very cold.

"Anyway, what seems to be the problem?" He asked, pen balanced between his fingers, waiting for our response.

"Well, this morning, he fell out of bed," Drew said. "And, hit his head on the nightstand. He has a little cut and we thought that was the extent of his injury, but he seems to be getting dizzy and he threw up just before we came here."

"When was that?"

Drew glanced at his watch. "About two hours ago."

The doctor nodded. "Have you had concussions in the past?"

"Yes. I'm a football player so I've had quite a few…"

"Hmm, alright. Well, we will get you some tests and see what happens. If you do have a concussion, then you'll need a two-week rest period. So, football will have to go on the backburner for now, son."

"Okay." Two weeks. That wasn't bad.

"I'll be right back." He announced before leaving the room.

Drew turned to face me. "Are you alright?"

"Yes." I chuckled.

"What?"

"Usually, I'm the one taking care of you. It's just nice to have things switched around for once."

"Well, believe it or not, I care about you."

My blush returned and just when I thought it was fading away...

Bashful, I avoided his gaze, looking down at my feet.

"And, I want you to be okay because I worry about you..." He stepped closer, resting a hand on my cheek. "You mean a lot to me, Joey." His thumb started to rub circles on my skin.

Without thinking, I leaned into his hand, craving his touch.

This broke the magic, causing him to pull away.

Dammit.

"What I mean is, I want you to be okay."

"Right," I said, lips becoming dry. "Well, let's just hope the test results come back negative..."

***

But, they didn't.

"It seems you have a concussion." The doctor said, looking over the charts.

"Are you sure?" Drew demanded.

The doctor looked up with an exasperated expression. "Yes, I'm sure, but if you'd like to try and do my job, please, be my guest."

He bit his tongue.

"As I was saying, you have a minor concussion. As I predicted, two weeks should be enough to get you back to normal. During those two weeks, I would advise that you take things easy. Don't do anything too strenuous. Avoid watching TV for too long. If you're in a setting with bright lights – including being out in the sun – make sure to wear sunglasses. Other than that, you can do your normal, everyday activities. Minus the football, of course." With a flourish of his hand, he signed the bottom of a document and handed it to me. "Here are my instructions printed out in written form. Don't forget them."

I took the paper, nodding slightly.

"You're free to go." He said, getting up and opening the door for us.

Drew helped me to my feet, still fretting over my every movement.

"I'm okay now," I told him. While I liked him pampering me, I didn't want to take advantage of him. "I can walk on my own."

"Oh, okay." Awkward, he pushed his hands into his pockets, starting on without me.

I trailed behind him.

Once I was inside his car, something felt off. The air was thick, and I immediately felt awkward. I glanced over at Drew, but he was looking at something, eyes distant.

Was he angry at me for declining his help?

Chapter 5

When we arrived at the hotel room, Drew immediately started to pack up his stuff.

He was acting really strange.

I couldn't shake the feeling that somehow, I had caused this.

Had I done something wrong?

"I think we should go." He said, suddenly looking at me with an intense gaze.

"What?"

"I think we should go."

"Go, where?" I asked, furrowing my brow in confusion.

"To Jamaica." He answered, tone serious.

"What?"

"I'm being serious. I mean, we won the honeymoon anyway. It would be a waste if we didn't go. Besides, the doctor said you needed two weeks of rest and relaxation. What better way to do that than on a tropical island?"

I hesitated. A part of me couldn't believe that Drew was actually suggesting this. I wet my lips, trying to get my mouth to work. "You do realize it's a honeymoon package, right?"

He nodded. "Yeah. That doesn't mean we have to do any of the romantic bits. We can just consider it a vacation. There's nothing wrong with two dudes going on vacation together, is there?"

"No, I guess not."

"Then, it's decided." He said with a smile. "Pack your bags and let's go."

"Right now?" I asked, eyes widening. "But, I only brought enough clothes for a couple of days. The honeymoon trip is two weeks..."

"You act as if you don't have the money to just buy a whole new outfit when you get there."

"That's true... but..."

"I don't want to hear any more buts out of you." He chided, wagging his finger in my direction. "We're going and that's final."

I knew that no matter what I said, I wouldn't win this battle, so I packed up my stuff, and before I knew it we were headed for our honeymoon.

***

"Wow..." I whispered as soon as we stepped into our hotel room. "This is... luxurious." We were on the top floor in one of the most expensive suites.

"Whoa... is that a hot tub on the veranda?" Drew marched forward, sliding open the glass doors. "We're definitely going to have to try that out later."

Wait.

Did he just say 'we'? Was he implying that we would go into the hot tub... together?

I grew excited just thinking about it.

Not wanting to embarrass myself with a boner, I stowed away in the bathroom, putting away my toiletries.

I couldn't believe this was happening. First, I had accidentally married my crush – a straight man who didn't know I was gay. And now, I was on a honeymoon with him.

Thinking it was too good to be true, I pinched myself.

I didn't wake up.

So, this wasn't a dream after all.

But, then again, it would never be the honeymoon I always wanted. This was just a... friendly... vacation. That's it. As much as I wanted to get emotions involved, they would have to stay on the sidelines. Probably forever.

The thought made me frown.

"Everything alright in here?" Drew asked, popping his head into the bathroom. "You look kind of upset."

"No, no, it's nothing."

"Are you sure? Is your head bothering you?"

"No. I'm okay. I promise."

He pressed his lips together, clearly unconvinced but he didn't push the subject. "Well, I just ordered us some room service. I thought we could enjoy some of those fancy appetizers and just chill for the rest of the night. I'm knackered. It's been a crazy day, don't you think?"

"Tell me about it." I agreed.

It was all turning into a blur. So much had happened in such little time that it was actually making my head spin.

"Alright, just come join me when you're done in here." He said before walking away.

I lingered in the bathroom for a little longer, just trying to gather my thoughts. There was something different about Drew. I couldn't quite put my finger on it but, he seemed more affectionate somehow. While we were on the plane, he had tucked me in with the complimentary blanket. And then, there was the fact that he kept stealing glances in my direction. Honestly, I didn't know what to make of it.

Maybe he was just tired.

In the end, I decided to change into my pajamas, so I'd be a bit more comfortable. Then, I headed out to the living room area, sitting down beside him.

Drew was looking very intensely at his phone.

"What's going on?" I asked.

"This..." He showed me the screen.

My heart stopped.

It was a picture of us... on the altar. Kissing.

And, it was all over the internet.

"It seems we are a trending topic..." He said, voice a bit hollow.

I barely registered what he said, too dazed by the photograph. We had kissed and, yet I couldn't remember it. Oh, how I yearned to know what his lips felt like, what they tasted like. Why couldn't I remember?

Damn it, alcohol, why do you have to ruin everything.

"I see..."

"We're overshadowing Henry... he was supposed to be the talk of the town... but we seemed to have stolen the show."

I nodded, not quite sure what to say.

Drew seemed eerily calm about the whole thing. I wanted to know exactly what he was thinking. Did he like the fact that we kissed, or did he hate it? Was he regretting going to Vegas with me or was he glad that things turned out the way they did?

These questions swirled around in my mind, making it hard to focus.

I just wanted to know what he felt.

"You know, everyone is fawning over us..."

"Huh?"

I looked up at him and he simply showed me some of the comments underneath our picture.

Aww, such a cute couple.

Congrats, guys. I hope it lasts for a long, long time.

This is what love looks like.

I'm glad to see a football player finally come out about his sexuality. This is beautiful.

The comments went on and on, most of them positive.

I was shocked. I had always assumed that people would judge and hate me for being gay but, so far, everyone seemed rather encouraging about it.

"What do you think about all this...?" I whispered, afraid to hear the answer but knowing I would go insane if I didn't know.

"What do I think?" He repeated. "I'm not sure yet... it's a lot to take in, you know? So, I'm not quite sure where I stand yet. What about you?"

I bit my lip.

He didn't like it.

I could already tell.

Well, there goes my hope that maybe, something could grow out of this...

"Yeah, I feel the same way." I lied, trying to sound convincing. "I think I need to sleep on it."

He nodded. "Good idea. Maybe we should just head to bed and let the internet explode without us."

"Right."

We both got up, heading toward the bedroom.

There, we awkwardly remembered that the room only had one bed – albeit a king-sized one, big enough for two, or three, or a dozen.

"Um, I'll just sleep on the couch," I said, not wanting to make things any weirder between us.

"No." He shook his head. "If anyone should sleep on the couch, it's me."

"No. I don't want you to do that. I mean, it's a big couch, but it's never as comfortable as sleeping on a bed."

We fell into silence, just looking at each other.

Finally, Drew stepped forward, slipping under the covers. "I guess our only solution is for us to share. I think it's big enough for the both of us so long as we stay on our separate sides."

I nodded. "Okay." Timidly, I joined him, staying precariously close to the edge.

"Goodnight." He said before turning his back toward me and turning off the light.

I blinked into the darkness, hands folded over my chest knowing it would be near impossible for me to fall asleep with Drew only a few feet away from me. I wanted nothing more than to destroy the distance between us and cuddle up against him, but I knew I would never have the guts to actually do that. So, I just laid there, barely moving, trying hard to remember what we did in bed on our wedding night.

Had we gone all the way?

Or had we simply fallen into bed together and passed out?

I wanted to know.

But, as much as I grappled in the dark, it was clear that Drew wasn't interested. He was still keeping his distance, clinging to his identity as a straight man. And yet, he wasn't reacting the way I thought he would.

He seemed to have accepted our marriage and what people thought about it.

Was he okay pretending to be gay? Or did he not care?

Maybe dealing with internet drama was too petty for him.

I didn't know, and it killed me.

Eventually, I fell asleep, tossing and turning for most of the night.

***

But, when I woke up, there were a pair of strong arms wrapped around me. I tensed, holding my breath.

Could it be?

I dared to look up, finding Drew's sleeping face only inches away from mine.

My heart skipped a beat.

God, he was handsome.

There was no way a guy like him could like someone like me, gay or not. He was way out of my leagues and I've always known it. But, a man can dream, can't he?

Savoring the moment, I kept as still as possible, trying not to wake him.

As I laid there, his intoxicating scent wafted up to my nose. He had a masculine scent that caused a rush of excitement to course through my veins.

Fuck, he was sexy.

I knew that if I stayed there any longer, I might end up doing something I would later regret. So, I tried to wiggle out of his embrace but as soon as I started to move, he tightened his grip, like he didn't want to let me go.

Then, his eyes opened. He looked down at me and smiled. "Mmm..." He mumbled, still half asleep. Slowly, he leaned down until our foreheads were touching. "Morning..."

"Morning..." I whispered back, my heart rocketing inside my chest.

He rubbed his nose against mine.

I held my breath as his lips grew closer and closer.

But then, suddenly, he snapped out of his stupor, jerking away. "Sorry..." He said quickly, running his fingers through his hair.

I couldn't hide the disappointment on my face. I had been so close to kissing him. Why hadn't I just leaned forward and done it?

Quickly, he got out of bed and locked himself in the bathroom.

I sighed.

This would never work...

He was probably already counting down the days until our divorce.

Yet, when he came out of the bathroom, he didn't look upset. Instead, he looked rather refreshed, flashing me his charming white smile. "What are you doing? Get dressed, we're going to the beach."

It was only then that I realized he was wearing nothing other than his swim trunks.

I bit my lip, trying to keep my excitement in check but I could already feel my body reacting to the sight of him. Blood rushed from my head down to my cock. It sprung to attention, nearly pitching a tent in the sheets.

"Um... okay," I answered. "Just... um... give me a minute."

He tilted his head in question but to my relief, he walked away, leaving me alone.

I let out the breath I was holding.

Phew, that was a close one.

With my cock still raging and begging for attention, I headed for the bathroom, taking a quick shower before I tossed on my swim trunks.

Drew was already waiting for me in the dining room. "I ordered us some breakfast. I can't really member the last time we ate properly." He handed me a glass of orange juice. "Don't worry, it's just plain juice. No alcohol." He chuckled. "We don't need a repeat of our wedding night." As he said that, his eyes almost seemed to twinkle.

Or, was I just imagining that?

With my mind racing, trying to interpret his words, I sat down, sipping on the tropical drink. "Mmm, this is good."

"Isn't it. There's a splash of mango in there that makes it to die for."

I took another sip before finally putting it down and turning to my omelet. "This looks good as well."

"Well, I know you like cheese omelets, so I got you one."

"You actually remembered that?"

"You know, I do pay attention even if it doesn't seem that way."

"I never said that you didn't... I'm just surprised. It's such a trivial thing."

"Well, like I said, I care about you. Besides, we're married now. I'm supposed to know these things." He said with a wink.

"Right." My cheeks were turning red.

He was being exceedingly affectionate this morning.

What had gotten into him?

***

When we were done, we headed for the beach, finding a nice shady spot underneath a palm tree. In front of us, the water was the color of crystal, sparkling in the sunlight.

Families frolicked in the water while couples teased each other. In a way, I was envious of them. I wanted that too.

I glanced over at Drew who had turned over and fallen asleep.

Maybe, just maybe, he'd warm up to the idea. In fact, it seemed to be happening already.

Mr. and Mr. Cohen.

I quite liked the sound of that. It had a certain ring to it.

Before I could continue my fantasies, someone approached our lawn chairs. They were holding a microphone in their hands.

A reporter.

So, they had found us already.

Great, just great.

So much for rest and relaxation.

Quickly, I shook Drew, knowing he would want to be awake for this.

He started, looking around, slightly disoriented before his gaze fell on me. "What's wrong?" He mumbled, voice husky from sleep.

"A reporter," I said, subtly jutting my thumb in their direction.

"Already?"

"Yeah."

"Crap."

We straightened up in our seats, looking at the young woman.

"Hello, I'm sorry to bother you but I'm from Gixapex News. We've been following the development of your relationship and we would just like to get a few words about your honeymoon so far and maybe a picture we can put in the paper." She spoke with a soft cadence that made it easy to trust her. I could understand why she was a reporter.

"Sure," Drew answered for us. "What would you like to know?"

I looked at him, a bit surprised by his willingness to participate. Something about this didn't seem right. If he came out and said that he was married, to a man, wouldn't that ruin his chances with women? I thought again about all the girls he used to bring home when we were in college together. If he publicly announced he was unavailable, all that would be thrown out the window.

A part of me was happy about that, but at the same time, I couldn't help but wonder what he was up to.

Something was definitely brewing in that head of his and I wish I knew what it was.

"Oh really? Thank you!" The reporter smiled brightly. "Just give me a second. I won't take up more than fifteen minutes of your time." She pulled out a small notepad from her bag, flipping through the pages. "Ah, here we are. Okay, I just have a few questions."

"Go on." Drew prompted, almost eager to answer.

"What made you two decide to tie the knot?"

Drew smiled fondly before wrapping an arm around my waist. "Well, we have been thinking about it for a while now. When we were in Vegas, we just couldn't wait any longer. We knew it was the right time."

The woman fed off his words, eyes shining brightly.

I couldn't believe my ears.

He was downright lying.

But, why?

It didn't make any sense.

What was he going to gain from all this? As I tried to wrap my head around the whole thing, Drew continued to answer her questions. He didn't hesitate, he didn't bat an eyelash. It was almost like he had rehearsed all this.

"What about you, Mr. Cohen?" She giggled. "How does it feel to be a married man?"

"Um..." I looked at her, gasping for words, like a fish out of water. "Well..." I continued to struggle, trying to figure out what to say.

"Don't mind my Joey. He can be a little bashful." Drew pulled me into a tighter embrace. "I can say, with great confidence, that we are very happy together. Aren't we, honey?"

Before I could say a word, he leaned forward and kissed me.

I was taken by such surprise that I didn't even move. My body was stiff as his lips continued to press against mine, waiting for a reaction.

The reporter quickly scrambled out her camera, taking picture after picture.

As the kiss intensified, I forgot she existed. I simply melted into my husband. With my eyes closed, it felt like the whole world had come to a stop. Everyone else had vanished and the only people left were me and him. It was perfect. Naturally, I wrapped my arms around his neck, letting my fingers tangle into the back of his hair, tugging on it softly.

God, this felt so good.

It was everything I dreamed it would be and so much more.

I savored it, addicted to his sweet taste. I felt like I would never be able to get enough of him.

He pulled me closer, our bodies locking together.

Fuck.

If he kept this up, I was sure to get excited.

But, before things could get too spicy, he pulled away, leaving me wanting more.

Much more.

Chapter 6

After the reporter left, I remained in a daze.

What had just happened?

Had Drew just kissed me?

My lips still tingled. I touched them ever so gently.

Was I dreaming?

At this point, I didn't even know anymore.

"Is something wrong?" Drew asked, having moved back to his own lawn chair as if none of that had ever happened. How was he so cool and collected right now? I tried to read his face but there was nothing written there. His eyes were like two blank slates, making it impossible for me to figure out what he was thinking.

"Why'd you kiss me?" I finally asked.

"Because it felt right."

"You mean... you wanted to kiss me."

He smirked. "Of course."

My heart thumped like ever before. "Does that mean... you like me?"

"I married you, didn't I?" His answers were quick and confident.

Somehow, he had done a full 360 from the morning we woke up naked together. What had caused this? Did he genuinely have feelings for me or was it something else? I couldn't help but feel suspicious. All my life, I had known Drew as a straight womanizer. He prided himself on the fact that he could seduce any woman he saw and yet, here he was, pretending to be in love with me. But, what if he wasn't pretending?

"I don't get it..."

"What is there not to get?" He asked, sitting back down beside me, taking my cheeks into my hands. "I'm not blind, Joey. I've known that you've had a crush on me for a long time."

"You what?" I nearly choked on my words. "H-How?"

"It was pretty obvious. All this time and not one girlfriend? I had my doubts and then one day, in the locker room, I noticed the way you were looking at me. There was lust in your eyes and from that moment forward, it was impossible not to notice the way you acted around me."

"I..." I blushed like crazy. "How long have you known?"

"A few years now." He answered.

"Why didn't you say anything?"

"I was waiting for you to come out. I didn't want to expose you if you weren't comfortable with your sexuality."

"But... wait... does that mean that you're...?"

"Gay... no."

"Then, how?"

He sighed. "I'm not sure. I'm not attracted to other men... but with you, it's different. Does that make me gay? Maybe. But, at the same time, I still like girls. So, bisexual? But, what's the point in putting a label on it? I like you and that's that." He flashed his signature smile before leaning forward and kissing my nose. "Don't look so surprised."

"I just... this is a lot to take in."

"Well, if you don't want to be my husband, we can still get the divorce."

"No, no." I shook my head. "That's not what I mean. It's just that the morning after we got married, you were so adamant about getting our marriage nullified. I thought you were grossed out about being with me or something."

He stopped me from talking by pressing his lips to mine. I tried to continue but he made me melt the instant he held me into his chest. Helpless, I wrapped my arms around him, vowing to never let him go.

Whatever was happening, it didn't make any sense but there was no point in me trying to ruin a good thing. Maybe he had changed. I wasn't about to complain.

All too soon, he pulled away. "Mmm, that's nice." He mused before locking his fingers with mine and hoisting me to my feet. "What do you say we take a little dip. I've been dying to get in the water."

"Okay," I said, a bit too dazed to think properly.

Together, we walked down the sandy beach until our toes hit the water. There, we lingered a while, just enjoying the beautiful sight and the salt air against our faces. Drew continued to hold my hand, squeezing it gently, as if to tell me he wouldn't let go.

"Are you ready?"

"Do you think it's going to be cold?" I asked.

"I don't think so." He answered and then before I could react, he was running into the water with me in tow.

I stumbled after him, nearly faceplanting into the sand but I managed to regain my balance.

We kept running until we were chest deep.

"Ah, this is perfect." He moaned, tilting his head back and letting his body float onto the surface. "Can we stay on honeymoon permanently?"

I laughed, finally coming to accept the fact that maybe this was real after all. I pushed all my doubts out of my head and waded over to my husband, splashing water in his direction.

He instantly straightened himself out, giving me the evil eye. "Oh! You're going to regret that!" Suddenly, he dove into the water, disappearing from sight.

Shit.

I looked at my feet, trying to spot him but it was too late.

He grabbed hold of my ankles and dragged me under.

I sunk like a rock, hitting the sandy bottom.

There, Drew grabbed me and pulled into yet another kiss.

My head spun with happiness.

This was heaven on earth.

I just prayed that it wouldn't all come crashing down around me. I wanted this to last forever.

And then some.

Chapter 7

On our fourth day, we decided to hit up the jet skis. I was actually a little nervous. I had never done anything water-sport related before. Plus, I wasn't that great of a swimmer. I much preferred to have solid earth beneath my feet.

Still, Drew convinced me, saying that it would be a lot of fun. Besides, he promised he would drive and keep me safe – no matter what.

That alone had been enough to comfort me.

"This is going to be awesome." He said as we headed down the docks. "I can't believe you've never been jet skiing before. It's a lot of fun."

I shrugged. "I never really lived by the water. Never got the chance to try."

"Well, you're going to try now."

The instructor brought us to two jet skis. "Wait... why are there two...? I thought I was riding with you."

"Well... I might have lied about that."

I gulped. "I don't know about this."

"Oh, come on, don't be such a baby. You're a star quarterback for one of the best teams in the league. A lot of people look up to you. You're a role model. And yet, you're scared of a jet ski. Come on, it's not even that hard."

I bit my lip, hesitant.

"You know I'm not the best swimmer in the world."

"That's fine. We're wearing life jackets anyway. Stop worrying, everything will be okay. I promise." He kissed my lips ever so gently, offering me an encouraging smile.

I couldn't help but smile back.

Already, after a couple of days, he had managed to wrap me around his finger. We hadn't done anything other than kiss, but still, that alone felt like a lot. Besides, I didn't want us to rush into anything we weren't ready for. I didn't mind taking things slow if it meant this could last.

"Alright, I'll do it."

"Great." He chuckled. "But, don't expect me to go easy on you just because you're a newbie."

"Easy on me? What the hell are we doing out there?"

"Hoping some waves. Chasing some dolphins. You know, the usual."

"Dolphins?" I was starting to get nervous again, but I was already on the jet ski, the instructor pushing me off the dock. Gingerly, I pressed on the gas. It sprung forward in a jerky motion that took me by surprise. My stomach flew forward, nearly leaving my mouth.

Oh boy, this was going to be fun.

A second later, Drew zipped past me. "If you can catch me, maybe I'll make it worth your while tonight." He shouted with a wink.

My eyes widened.

Was he suggesting what I think he was suggesting?

At the thought of having him in a sexual context, I floored on the gas, whipping forward. I nearly lost my balance, but I managed to regain control, turning into the waves, following Drew's wake.

The water was calm for the most part, making my life a little bit easier. But, as soon as we hit the open water, everything changed. The waves became bigger and occasionally, I would end up jumping over one, catching air, and slamming back to the surface.

I'll admit, it wasn't the best experience in my life. Even with the adrenaline pumping through my veins, I didn't care for it.

In fact, I wanted to turn around and head back to the docks, but the thought of Drew's taunt kept me going. I wanted to know what he had in mind. I wanted to spend a night with him that didn't just end in us falling asleep on opposite sides of the bed.

I wanted more.

I wanted every inch of him, tangled up with every inch of me.

Distracted by these thoughts, I didn't pay quite enough attention to what I was doing.

Suddenly, I was flying high in the air. My grip loosened around the handlebars, making it completely impossible for me to maintain control.

And then, I went crashing down.

Hard.

Too hard.

The jet ski toppled over. The kill switch was ripped from its socket.

And, I went under, gulping in a lungful of water that made me choke.

If it wasn't for the life vest, I probably would have drowned, too disoriented to know which way is up and which way is down.

When I surfaced, I sucked in much-needed air, coughing hard, trying to expel the water from my lungs.

I was still suffering from my coughing fit when Drew jumped into the water after me. He had his hand on my life jacket, keeping me steady, even as the water bobbed us up and down. "Are you alright?" He asked, voice full of concern.

"Y-Yeah..." I managed to say.

"What happened?"

"I think I got a little too much air and I lost control."

He shook his head. "I'm sorry. I shouldn't have made you ride by yourself when you've never done it before. Do you want to ride back with me?"

"What about my jet ski?"

"The instructors will come back to get it. There's GPS on it. They'll find it."

"Are you sure?"

He nodded. "Yeah, I rather you be safe. Who cares about some stupid jet ski?" He smiled, leaning forward to kiss me but this one was different somehow – sweeter, maybe. Whatever it was, it sent a warmth throughout my whole body, making me feel like I could just float away.

Mmm.

He held me close for a moment before helping me onto the back of his jet ski.

A second later, he settled himself between my legs, taking control of the handlebars. "Make sure to hold on tight. This is going to be the ride of your life." He laughed, suddenly flying forward.

I held on for dear life as he jumped wave after water, getting some serious air. Despite what had just happened to me, I wasn't afraid. In fact, I felt safe and sound now that we were together. I smiled, leaning into him, praying that this happiness I felt deep in my heart would never fade away.

Chapter 8

All too soon, however, the honeymoon was over. Ruefully, we were forced to pack our bags and head back to the states.

"I can't believe it's over..." Drew said, grabbing our bags and heading out the door.

"Hold on," I said, rushing back into the bedroom and grabbing the disposable camera we had bought at one of the gift shops. We both had top of the line smartphones capable of taking stellar pictures but there was just something nostalgic about using an old camera like that. The pictures might come out crappy but in the end, it's the memory that really counts.

"What was all that about?" He asked after I returned. He was sipping on a bottle of root beer. "You want anything, by the way? They restocked the mini fridge. We might as well make use of it."

"What's in there?"

"Some soda, candy, mineral water. You know, the usual stuff."

I squatted down, browsing through my options. As I did so, I noticed Drew looking at me. There was something strange in his stare. His eyes were intense like he was seeing me for the very first time.

Suddenly, I became self-conscious.

"Um... is there something wrong?" I asked.

"What? No." He smiled.

"Why were you looking at me like that?"

"Is it a crime for a man to look at his husband?" He joked, walking up to me and wrapping his arms around my waist. But, there was something stiff about his embrace. Had it always been like this? I didn't know. Either way, I could tell that something was off.

"Drew, are you sure everything is alright?" I pressed.

"Of course, why wouldn't they be? I mean it's kind of sad we have to leave this place, but you have practice in two days anyway. If you stop playing, then we are both out of jobs, you know."

"Right." I nodded slowly. In that moment, it dawned on me that during our stay in Jamaica, Drew had focused a lot on money. It was strange. But, I decided to shrug it off. We were on vacation. It was normal for people to spend a bit more money. Maybe he had overspent and was a bit worried about it.

Whatever the reason, I'm sure it's nothing to get anxious about. I needed to learn just to let things run its course. I spent way too much time overthinking things. Maybe that's why I never expressed my feeling for Drew. I never thought it would end up like this.

"Anyway, we should probably hurry up or we're going to risk missing our flight."

"Alright. Alright." Quickly, I grabbed a bag of M&Ms and headed out the door.

While we were in the elevator, I waited for Drew to make a move. Odd. Usually, he at least gave me a kiss but not today.

Okay, maybe now was a good time to worry...

Things became even worse when we rode all the way to the airport in silence.

What was going on?

Was he giving me the cold shoulder?

Had I done something wrong?

***

After an agonizingly long time on the plane, we finally made it back home. Drew remained distant but every time I asked him about it, he claimed that everything was fine. So, I decided to just let it go. If I kept asking, he would just grow annoyed with me.

A few days passed.

I went back to practice.

The world went back to normal.

It was almost like nothing had happened and those two weeks with Drew had been nothing more than a vivid dream.

Except for the fact that we were bombarded with reporters every time we were seen in public together.

Today, Drew was sitting on the bleachers, watching us practice. When I looked up, reporters had somehow managed to infiltrate the field and flock around him, shoving microphones in his face. I didn't know how he could stand it.

I hated all the attention. It made me feel exposed. After all, reporters were skilled in invading your privacy.

"Bates! Get your head in the game!" Coach shouted, snapping me out of my trance. "Keep your eyes on the ball, not your little boy toy over there."

I gulped. "Yes, sir!" I took a deep breath and centered myself. As much as I liked Drew, football was my world. During the main season, I breathed, ate, and slept football. It was a part of every single minute of my day. With this newfound focus, I threw the perfect pass.

"Now, that's what I'm talking about! I want to see that sort of action on our opening game. Do you hear me?" He growled. "Now, do it again."

So, for the next two hours, I practiced pass after pass, getting drilled to pieces by the coach. By the time we were done, I was knackered.

Slowly, I shuffled my way toward the locker room with the rest of the team.

There, I shrugged off my sweaty uniform, ready to take a quick shower, but before I could grab my towel, Henry appeared right in front of me, a mean glower on his face. "I have a bone to pick with you?"

I stepped back. "What are you talking about?"

"You think I'm dumb or something?"

"Huh?"

"You planned to upstage my wedding, didn't you?"

"What... no. I don't even like all the attention."

He laughed. "Oh, that's a good one."

"I'm being serious. Drew is the one that answers all the interviews. I don't care for them."

"Why did you do it then? Couldn't you pick some other weekend?"

"Hey... it just happened."

"Yeah, sure." He clenched his teeth, stepping even closer. "I would just be careful if I were you. All this attention might get to your head and then someone might get hurt."

"Is that a threat?"

"Take it as you want." He said, slamming my locker with a loud thud.

As soon as he walked away, I couldn't help but feel like a high schooler all over again. Back then, I had constantly been picked on. If it wasn't for Drew, I probably would have gone home with a lot more black eyes than I did.

I shook my head.

Henry didn't scare me.

He was just angry that the coach was benching him for our first game after his arrest in Vegas. He claimed he didn't want any bad publicity for the team. Henry argued that the coach was out to get him.

But then, it hit me.

Publicity.

What if this was all about publicity.

No.

Drew wouldn't do that to me, would he?

But now the seed of doubt had been planted in my mind.

Did Drew marry me for me or for the fame and fortune?

Chapter 9

When I emerged from the locker room, Drew was gone, carried away to yet another interview. He didn't even bother to wait for me.

I sighed.

What I needed right now was to crawl into his arms. I just wanted him to hold me tight and tell me that everything was okay. That's all I wanted – all I needed.

But, I couldn't even have that.

So, I walked over to the parking lot, getting behind the wheel of my car.

I was the last one to leave so I decided to stay there a little while longer, making use of the peace and quiet. I needed the time to think.

While things with Drew were great, I just couldn't shrug off the feeling that something was wrong. It was simply too good to be true. At least, that's what I kept telling myself. I just couldn't accept the fact that Drew might genuinely like me.

No, that didn't make sense. He liked girls. I knew that. For a fact.

Countless times, I had heard him giving it to them through the thin walls of our college apartment.

How could he just forget about all that?

Sure, he could be bisexual but that, too, didn't feel right.

Maybe I should just stop worrying...

But, that's easier said than done. Once doubt creeps into your mind, it's practically impossible to push it out.

I bit my lip, leaning my head on the steering wheel, trying to figure out what I should do. The smart thing would be to talk to him but lately, he hasn't been one for talking. He'll just tell me everything is fine and flash a smile.

Sighing, I started the car and drove off.

About halfway through my commute, it started to rain. Or rather, downpour. Even after turning my wipers to full power, it wasn't enough to see properly.

I slowed down to a snail's pace, squinting through the rain.

Knowing I would only get hurt if I continued to drive, I pulled over into the breakdown lane, determined to wait it out. It wasn't like I had much else to do that evening.

But, as the minutes ticked by, I felt myself get bogged down by the weight of loneliness. So, I pulled my phone out of my pocket, deciding to send him a text.

Hey, where'd you go?

For a while, there was no response.

I just sat there, staring out the window at the rain, watching the occasional car drive by.

The rain became worse, mixing with lightning and thunder.

At this rate, I might end up stuck in my car all night.

I checked the weather report. Luckily, it said that the storm should let up in about an hour. Let's hope so, at least.

Sorry! One of the news channels wanted an interview with me. I hope you don't mind.

I stared at his text. That seemed to be the only thing he cared about. Interviews. Interviews. Interviews.

Again, the word publicity popped into my head.

No...

He wouldn't...

But, it was becoming more and more obvious.

He was using me.

That's what this was...

Joey, you there?

Yeah. I'm here.

Oh, okay. Where are you?

Pulled over on the side of the highway. I got trapped in the rain.

Do you want me to come get you?

No.

Okay, please drive slow then. I want you home in one piece. See you later!

I turned off my phone, putting it back in my pocket. Frustrated by this whole ordeal, I ran my fingers through my hair.

Maybe, it would just be best for the two of us if we got a divorce.

With this thought in mind, I started the car once more, pulling onto the highway, heading for city hall. There, I waited in line for the city clerk.

A few people recognized me, asking for my autograph.

I was happy to give it to them but when they started to ask me questions, my mood quickly soured.

"What does it feel like to be gay in such a masculine and straight community?" One man asked.

"What's it like to be married to your agent? Do you think there's a conflict of interest?" Came another.

"Please... I don't want to talk about this right now." I said, growing tense by all these people circling around me like vultures.

"Why don't you want to talk about it? Is there already some trouble brewing in your marriage?"

Who were all these people and why did they think they had the right to know every single detail of my personal life.

I hated it.

Finally, I reached the front of the line.

The clerk was an older woman with fluffy white hair and red-rimmed glasses. "How may I help you?" She addressed me like I was just an everyday person.

Good.

At least she wouldn't give me a hard time about all this. "I would like the papers needed to file a divorce."

She cocked an eyebrow in my direction, studying my face with her blurry blue eyes. In the end, however, she got off her chair and headed toward a filing cabinet. She searched through it for a few moments before returning with a thick packet. "You know, most people just fill this out online now." She handed it through the partition. "Do you have your marriage license? You'll need it."

I nodded.

"Then, just fill out the packet, send it in, and you should be all set. Do you have any questions?"

"No."

"Alright, have a nice day."

Well, that was easier than I thought.

As I walked out of the building, however, an enormous wave of guilt washed over me. What was I doing? How could I file for a divorce when I didn't know the truth behind Drew's intentions? This felt like I was going behind his back...

Still, I carried it out of my car. At least, if I decided to get the divorce, I already had the needed documents.

Driving home, the storm continued to rage with wind and rain pelting against my car, making it hard to control.

Everything was fine, however, until, out of nowhere, a car rammed into me.

The next this I knew, I was flying off the side of the highway, straight into the surrounding woods. In an instant, the hood of the car turned into an accordion, scrunching in on itself. My body slammed forward, crashing through the windshield.

I had been dumb enough to forget my seatbelt.

And now, here I was, bleeding and alone on the side of the road.

I groaned in pain, feeling like every bone in my body had been shattered in two. I tried desperately to fish my phone out of my pocket, but my fingers barely moved, covered in my own blood.

Smoke billowed from the car.

This wasn't happening.

This was some sort of nightmare.

But the pain was real.

It burned every inch of my body, making it hard to breathe.

Biting my lip, I pushed past the pain, finally moving my arm just enough to grab my phone. The screen was cracked and the phone itself bent but at least it was still working. With shaking fingers, I managed to call Drew's number, putting it on speaker.

It rang and rang and rang.

Please, for the love of God, pick up.

It rang and rang and rang.

I could already feel myself growing faint.

If this didn't work, I wouldn't have the strength to make another phone call. I would probably die here.

Please, Drew, pick up the phone.

To my relief, my prayers were answered.

"Hello?"

"Drew... I..." My mouth felt incredibly dry making it hard to speak. "Drew... I... crashed. The car is totaled... I don't know how much longer I can hold on... but I have to tell you something..."

"What? No! Don't talk like that. I'm going to come get you right now. Where are you? Joey... where are you?" He shouted through the phone.

I took a deep breath, blinking through the pain that threatened to consume me.

"I love you, Drew."

Chapter 10

The darkness was all consuming. Everywhere I looked, there it was, wrapping tighter and tighter around my body.

I would give anything to make it go away but it was persistent, making the world move in slow motion.

Was this the afterlife?

The question kept me moving – or rather, wading – through the black sludge. There had to be a way out of this.

I refused to believe that this was the end.

But, after what felt like an eternity of shifting through nothingness, I settled down and closed my eyes.

Instantly, Drew appeared, standing there with his bright smile.

When I opened my eyes, he was gone.

Ah, he's just a fantasy, like he's always been.

I hugged my knees to my chest, resting my head on top of them before closing my eyes once more.

If my imagination is the only place where I can properly be with him, then I guess I'll just have to live inside my head.

There, he walked over to me and folded me into his arms, resting my head on his chest.

I smiled, soaking in his warmth, trying to bottle it up and keep it forever.

He held me for a long, long time running his hand up and down my back in a soothing motion.

"Mmm…" I mumbled. "Don't ever leave me."

"Why would I leave you?" He whispered, looking down at me. "You know how much I care about you."

I bit my lip.

"You don't believe me, do you?" There was such sincerity in his eyes that it made my heart ache to have ever doubted him.

Why had I been so stupid?

Of course, he loved me. He always has. I was just too blind and paranoid to ever notice it.

All those girls... they didn't mean anything.

They never did.

He was just as scared as I was about coming out.

I just never realized it.

He smiled down at me. "Now you get it." He kissed the top of my head.

But, then he started to fade away. I tried to chase after him to no avail. He was just out of grasp, leaving me alone in the darkness once more.

"No!" I screamed at the top of my lungs, but no one answered me. "Please... come back..." I begged, tears streaming down my cheeks.

I had made a huge mistake and now I would never be able to fix it.

My heart felt like it was breaking into a million pieces, each one stabbing into my chest.

If only I could just wake up...

I slammed my fists forward, trying to get rid of my anger but all I managed to do was lose my balance and stumble forward.

Suddenly, I was falling.

Fast.

I braced myself for an impact, but it never came.

Slowly, I opened my eyes.

They were bombarded by a bright white light that immediately made me close then again. Then, sliver by sliver I managed to open them properly, looking up at a white, sterile looking ceiling.

Where was I?

When I turned my head, my heart skipped a beat.

There he was.

Drew.

I smiled but that smile instantly vanished the second I saw what he was holding in his hands.

The divorce papers.

Shit.

Ever so gently, I tried to sit up, but an agonizing stab of pain shot through my body, forcing me to take a sharp intake of breath.

Drew's eyes flew open.

"You're awake…" He whispered.

Before I knew what was happening, he launched forward, wrapping his arms around me.

Again, pain radiated through my body. I winced.

"Sorry…" He pulled away quickly. "I didn't mean… Are you okay? Do you need me to call a nurse?"

I shook my head. "No…" My voice was cracked and gravelly like I had been asleep for a very long time. It hurt to talk but still, I tried. I needed answers. "What happened?"

Drew frowned. "You were in an accident. A pretty bad one. The doctors say it's a miracle that you're alive…"

"I see…" I looked away, seeing the worry in his eye. It killed me inside. I was the cause of that pain and I hated it.

"I'm just glad you're okay. When I saw the condition you were in… I thought for sure that I was going to lose you…" There were tears in his eyes.

It was the first time I had ever seen him cry.

He really did care about me.

Why had I ever doubted him?

"I'm so sorry…" I whispered, too shamefaced to look at him.

We were quiet for a moment, neither one of us saying a word.

I wanted to hide away – to disappear – but I was helplessly bound to that hospital bed. A plethora of needles was protruding from my skin.

Eventually, I couldn't stand the silence any longer. "How long have you been here?" I asked, daring to look up at him.

"I haven't left your side for a second."

I wet my lips. "How long have I been out for?"

"Two days."

I looked at him, eyes widening in disbelief. "You stayed all that time."

"Of course." He said, sitting back down. "There's something I need to tell you too, Joey."

I held my breath.

"I love you."

My heart soared at those words. All the pain in my body just melted away.

He loved me!

"But, there's one thing I have to know…" He looked down like he regretted having to ask this question. "Why was this in your car?" He held up the divorce papers.

"I…" Suddenly, my throat felt like it was swelling shut, making it hard to breathe. I wanted to tell him everything, but I feared what he would think.

"Just tell me the truth, Joey."

I looked at him with pleading eyes, hoping he would let this go but of course, he didn't.

So, I took a deep breath and did my best to explain. "I just couldn't accept the fact that you liked me. All my life, I've known you as a straight guy. Never in my wildest dreams did I think I ever really had a chance with you. Yes, I had a massive crush on you. I always had. But, I always reminded myself that it was just a crush – a fantasy that I would never get to live out to fruition. Then, we got married. At first, you were in such a rage about it. I thought I disgusted you. That's why you were pushing the divorce so hard. But then, you had a sudden change of heart. I didn't know what to make of it. So, I started coming up with all these crazy theories. I got paranoid. I just thought… that may be… you were using me for publicity. I know that sounds horrible… please don't hate me." By the time I was done, I found myself breathless.

He looked at me for a long time before he moved from the chair to the edge of the bed. "If I'm completely honest with you, I have my own confession to make. Your theory was partially true. When we were first married, I was devastated. I was so rooted in my identity as a straight man that I couldn't accept being anything else. That's why I wanted the divorce. And then, Jenkins gave me a call. He said that he wanted to use the marriage to the team's advantage or he would kick you off and replace you with someone else. So, I started acting all romantic and loving in front of the interviewers, so they'd think we were in a healthy relationship. But, as time wore on, it wasn't just an act anymore. I genuinely came to love you. A lot."

I couldn't believe my ears.

All this time... he was just trying to protect me. It was never his own selfish motives.

Why did I ever suspect him of such?

I felt horrible just knowing I harbored that doubt.

"So... do you still want to divorce me?" He asked.

I shook my head. "I never wanted to divorce you. I was just scared..."

"Well, there's no reason for you to be scared anymore. We have each other." He said with a smile. "And nothing is ever going to tear us apart."

***

Six months later.

I was finally fully recovered from my accident. With a note from my doctor, I was free to resume my daily activities, including football.

Still, Drew had gotten into the habit of pampering me.

When we arrived at the house, he got out of the car and opened my door for me, a smile on his face.

It melted my heart like it always did.

"You know, you don't have to keep opening the door for me. I can do it myself now."

"I do it because I like to." He said, kissing the top of my head. "I like doing nice things for you because I like you. I love to see you smile."

His words made me blush.

He chuckled, leaning down to kiss my lips.

"Mmm..." I mumbled as I wrapped my arms around his neck, tangling my fingers in his hair. No matter how much we made out, his lips were still as addicting as the first day I tasted them.

I pulled him closer, hips grinding against his, breathing becoming ragged.

God, he had a way of making me excited.

Sometimes, it was hard to control. Very hard. Literally.

Breathless, he pulled away, looking at me with this naughty glint in his eye. "You know, with the doctor's clearance, that means you can do pretty much anything..."

I smirked. "Does that mean I can do you..."

"If that's what you want..." he said in an almost innocent tone. "I mean, I'm not going to complain if my sexy husband wants to fuck me."

I chuckled. "Then, what are we doing?"

Giggling, we ran into the house.

Before I knew what was happening, he swept me off my feet, cradling me against his chest, as he carried me up the stairs – no easy feat given I was a well-built football player. But, Drew didn't even break a sweat, bounding up the stairs, obviously eager to get me in bed.

We had both been waiting for this moment for months now. It was torturous trying to wait when our lust for each other seemed to grow more and more intense with each passing day.

I couldn't help it.

Drew was sexy as fuck.

Once we were in the bedroom, Drew threw me down on the mattress.

I rolled over, preventing him from pinning me down, playing hard to get.

He tried to tackle me down but again, I avoided him.

"Come here!" He yelled, trying to grab me. This time, he succeeded. With a fistful of my shirt in his hand, he ripped it right off my body, exposing my scar-filled chest.

I was a bit self-conscious about it now, but Drew didn't seem to mind.

Gently, he pushed me back, letting his lips dance along my skin, taking his time to kiss every single scar.

It made me shiver.

I never thought someone could love me this much, but every day Drew proved me wrong. He made me feel like I was the only man in the world – the only person he ever noticed.

We rolled over. I smiled down at him, my hands cupping his cheeks. "I love you," I whispered, unable to hide my emotions. "You make me so happy, you know that?"

"I'm glad."

As I leaned down, our lips collided together. When they touched, it was like fireworks exploding all around us.

I loved it. I craved it.

I needed more.

Our movements became desperate and horny as we ripped off each other's clothing, too eager to wait a moment longer.

As soon as my boxers came off, Drew smirked down at me. "Oh, I'm going to have so much fun with you, baby. Just sit back and enjoy the ride." He said with a wink.

Chapter 11

And damn, it was one hell of a ride.

He moved between my legs, letting his fingertips glide across my thighs, sending goosebumps all over my body. Begging for it, I lifted my hips into the air, cock twitching in anticipation.

But, he wasn't ready to give me what I wanted just yet.

His fingers continued to dance, spreading my legs inch by inch. Occasionally, he would look up at me with this naughty look on his face. He knew exactly what he was doing to me – winding me up like a toy, pushing me toward the edge of insanity.

I loved it.

Already, I was becoming breathless and it only became worse when he added his lips to the mix, trailing along my thighs getting closer and closer to my member.

Desperate for stimulation, I reached down, grabbing my shaft in my hand, rubbing it slowly.

He watched me with hungry eyes but didn't move to help me.

Instead, his lips lingered just left of my balls, teasing me with the possibility.

I tensed, just waiting for it.

And, he didn't disappoint.

As soon as his lips made contact, I nearly lost it. Biting my lip, I held back the wave of pleasure coursing through my body. No, I couldn't cum just yet. I wanted to make this moment last as long as physically possible.

Slowly, he swirled his tongue all around me, flooding me with ecstasy.

"How much do you want it?" He asked, looking up at me with devilish eyes.

"Bad..." I breathed. "So bad." I tangled my fingers in his hair, desperately wanting to feel his hot mouth against my girth.

He smirked. "That's not very convincing."

"Drew... please... don't do this to me. I want it so bad..." I pushed my hips into the air, hoping he would pity me.

Luckily, he did.

To my great pleasure, he wrapped his lips around me, letting his tongue swirl around the tip, flicking back and forth until I thought I would lose my mind.

"Oh... that feels so good..." I trembled, pushing my hips forward, letting it slide further into his mouth. "That's it, baby..."

As he pushed himself, his tongue continued to slide along the underside of my cock, making the blowjob a thousand times better.

Oh, this was definitely worth all the wait.

Suddenly, he picked up the pace, bobbing his head up and down, hips pressed tightly against me, mouth open wide, sucking hard.

"Fuck..." I moaned, toes curling. "That's amazing!" I shouted, head tilting back, eyes rolling into my skull.

I had never felt anything like this before. I never wanted it to stop.

So, I kept moving my hips, falling into perfect sync with him.

He held onto my thighs, deep throating me down. My cock slid down his throat, feeling him gag and choke around my thickness.

It was so hot.

But, all too soon I lost control, cum exploding from the tip.

Eagerly, he lapped up every drop, looking at me with great big eyes, almost like he wanted more.

Licking his lips, he sat up, smirking at me. "Now, my turn." He growled, turning me over.

He snuck his arm underneath my waist, placing me on all fours. "Mmm..." I moaned, enjoying the view from our headboard mirror. Drew looked so sexy hovering over me like that. I wanted him to take control of every each of me. And from the devilish look in his eye, he was going to do just that.

Slowly, he pressed his tip against my entrance, taking his time to tease me.

I rocked against him, wishing he would just plunge into my depths but, of course, he didn't.

Instead, he reached into our nightstand and pulled out a bottle of lube.

When did that get there?

It seems like Drew had prepared for this night.

The thought made me even more excited.

The lube was cold against my hole but that quickly left my mind as soon as I felt his fingers probing into me. He pushed in his middle finger first, pumping it in and out of me at a methodical pace that would never get me off but would keep me on edge for a very long time.

"Do you like that?" He whispered into my ear, pulling at my hair to tilt my head back.

"God, yes." I breathed, heart pounding. "I love it..."

"Do you want more?"

"Yes."

"How much more?"

"All of you."

"Can you handle that."

"Only one way to find out." I countered, a smirk forming on my face.

I loved how naughty we were getting.

"You asked for it." He pulled my hair a little harder, jamming two of his fingers inside my tight hole. He wiggled them around, loosening me up. Then, he added a third.

Already, I felt like I was being stretched to my limit. It didn't hurt but there was a significant pressure. I squirmed under his touch, hoping to feel his cock soon. I didn't know how much longer I'd be able to wait.

"So eager..." He whispered, kissing the side of my neck as he moved back to his middle finger, teasing me with how slow he was going.

This was torture.

Sweet, sweet torture.

His kissed continued to the nape of my neck before following the curve of my spine. When he reached the middle of my back, he pulled away altogether.

I whimpered.

Why had he stopped?

"Drew..."

Suddenly he took my cock in his hand, stroking it hard and fast.

I moaned, back arching in pleasure, fingers curling around the sheets, just trying to steady myself.

With his other hand, he pushed me down, so I was in a face down ass up position.

And then, he rammed right into me.

Every single inch.

Fuck.

It felt so good...

For a few seconds, he didn't move, just letting me grow accustomed to his huge cock impaled deep inside of me.

I was breathing hard, just trying to fathom what was going on.

Never in my wildest dreams did I imagine this would feel so good.

Soon, I would become an addict.

I probably already was.

"Fuck me, baby," I begged.

And, he did just that.

Grabbing me by the hips, he went to town, slamming into me over and over again.

I moaned out, screaming his name, my hole tightening around him.

He added some more lube to the mix, making it easier for me.

"Mmm... you're so tight..." Still, he continued to thrust into me, working like a well-oiled piston.

Already, I could feel my balls tightening with an impending orgasm.

Oh God, not yet. I didn't want the night to be over.

But, the way Drew was fucking me, he was going to make quick work out of me.

"I'm going to cum!" I shouted.

"Then, cum for me..." He whispered into my ear, nibbling the lobe ever so gently.

Almost on cue, the second round of cum erupted onto the bed cover. I nearly collapsed, overwhelmed by the feeling caused by two back to back orgasms.

"Fuck..." I sighed, legs giving out.

Soon after, I felt Drew's warm, sticky cum shooting onto my back. "Ahh..." he breathed, laying down beside me with a dirty smirk on his face. "That was amazing."

I smiled back, leaning forward to kiss him. "Damn, I knew that would be good... but I didn't think it would be that good."

"Hey, what's that supposed to mean?" Drew pouted slightly as he grabbed a fresh hand towel, cleaning me up. With a skilled throw, he tossed it into the clothes hamper.

"Don't take that the wrong way. It was supposed to be a compliment."

"Sure. Sure." He laughed, plopping back down on the mattress, staring up at the ceiling. "You know, when I was younger, I never even dreamt of being in love with another man but now that I have you in my life, I wouldn't want it any other way."

"You're going to make me blush." I protested.

"Too late. You're already as red as a tomato."

Bashfully, I hide my face in his chest.

He chuckled, running his fingers through my hair.

I moaned ever so slightly, enjoying his touch. "Mmm, that feels so good. You have a really nice touch."

"Do I?"

"Mhm."

He kissed the top of my head. "I'm glad you like it because there's a lot more where that came from. I'm not done with you yet."

My eyes widened. "You mean, there's more?"

"Much more."

"I don't know about that."

"You don't have a choice." He growled, rolling on top of me and pinning me to the bed. "You're mine and I'm going to do whatever I want with you." When he finished, he leaned down, biting into the side of my neck, leaving behind a very noticeable hickey. Now all the world would know.

He smirked before getting off me and pulling me into his arms. "I like you."

"I like you too."

"How much?"

"A lot," I said, gently kissing his chest before resting my head on it. Mmm, he was so comfy. Already, I could feel my body melting into his.

"You know, I'm glad I married you."

"I'm glad I married you too. That might be the one and only time I'm glad I got drunk."

He laughed. "Right, or we'd still be pretending to be 'just friends.' And, I'd still be pretending to be straight."

"Well, technically, aren't you still straight?"

"No. I'm attracted to you. I don't care about girls at this point. All that matters is you. If we want to put a label on it, technically I'm gay."

"But, who needs labels. We don't need to fit into any of society's molds so long as we have each other. Right?"

"Right." He tightened his arms around me, pulling me tighter until we fit together like two puzzle pieces. I liked how our bodies seemed to be made for each other.

"I love you..." I whispered.

"I love you too."

"This is nice."

"Very nice." He continued to run his fingers through my hair.

I nearly purred, my body arching with pleasure. "How do you do it?" I asked.

"Do what?"

"Every time I see you, my heart just beats out of control. We've been together for six months and I still get butterflies whenever you're with me. I guess a part of me still thinks that this is all a dream."

"Why would you think that?" He cocked an eyebrow in question.

"Because you're way too good for me. You could do so much better."

Suddenly, he had my face in his hands. "I don't want anything better. You're perfect. And, I love you."

I blushed. "Really?"

"Yes. I really do love you. And..." He paused, pinching me hard. "... that's your proof that I'm real. But, if you still don't believe me, they say that you can never see a clock in your dreams." So, he pointed across the bedroom at our grandfather clock, pendulum moving back and forth. "So, like it or not, you're stuck with me for a very long time."

Smiling, I rolled on top of him, straddling him, hands on his chest. "I like it. I like it a lot." As I spoke, my hand slipped down his body, finding his now limp cock. After a few strokes, it was already at full mast. My smirk deepened. "Are you ready for round two, baby?"

"Oh, I'm always ready."

Before I knew it, he had flipped me over, taking control. "But, I wasn't kidding when I said you were mine and that I'm going to do whatever I want to you tonight."

My heart skipped a beat.

Just when I thought this man couldn't get any sexier he just had to prove me wrong.

God, I loved it.

Epilogue

Five years later.

"And Bates lines up to make the throw. He's aiming at wide receiver Butler. Will he make it?"

A pause. The whole stadium holds its breath, waiting for the fateful moment when the football flies from my fingertips and soars over the field.

Not this time.

At the very last second, I clutched the ball to my chest and ran forward, making a sly pass to one of my teammates who instantly sprung into action, whipping past the unsuspecting team.

"We've never seen anything like this, folks! It's a complete fake out and the Hawks fell for it. The Kites might just have this in the bag..."

Again, another pause.

"And, that's it. Douglas is in the end zone! With only a few minutes left in the fourth quarter, there isn't much for the Hawks to do..."

I smirked to myself, knowing we had just won the championship.

***

"You did great out there!" Drew was ready to greet me the second I stepped out of the locker room. He enveloped me in a hug, kissing me passionately, taking my breath away. "I knew you could do it. How many rings do you have now?" He asked with a smirk on his face.

"Four and next year, I'm going to make it five. Just you wait and see."

"You better, or else, no celebratory sex for you," Drew said with a wink.

"Oh, it's a done deal now. There's no way I'm missing out on that."

We both laughed, getting into the car.

Drew had insisted on driving. Ever since my accident, he's been iffy about letting me get behind a wheel.

"Are we just going home and straight to bed or...?"

"Oh, no, I have plans for us."

"You do?"

"Mhm." There was a mischievous glint in his eyes.

He was definitely up to something. I could almost taste it.

"Aren't you going to ask what we're doing?" He asked, glancing over at me.

"I figure if I just wait long enough, I'll find out. I'm a pretty patient person. I can wait."

He looked at me, shaking his head.

"You really want to tell me, don't you?"

"Yes."

"Alright, what are our plans for tonight?"

"I'm not telling you." He grinned, adjusting his grip on the wheel, a look of smugness all over his face.

"You're such a punk sometimes."

"You love it, don't even lie." He chuckled.

"I do." I reached over, resting my hand on his thigh, giving it a nice squeeze. "So, you're really not going to tell me?"

"Nope. Because if I do, you're not going to stick around."

"Uh-oh. I don't like the sound of that." Already, I had a million different scenarios in my head. Drew could have planned anything.

This was making me nervous.

"Don't worry. It's nothing bad."

"You know, I don't really trust you right now."

He gasped, feigning offense. "How could you say that after five years together..."

"Five years and six months, but who's keeping track?" I said, trying to sound nonchalant.

"Anyway, we'll be there in twenty minutes."

It was the longest twenty minutes of my life.

I kept watching the road, trying to figure out our destination but so far, I was completely in the dark.

Finally, he pulled into a small dirt road.

"Uh... Drew..."

"Don't worry."

I was definitely worried.

After a very bumpy ride, we reached the ocean. Up ahead was a dinky looking dock, housing a jet ski.

"Oh no... not this again."

"Yes. This again. It'll be much better this time. I promise. I'll drive, and the water is calm. I made sure to check the forecast. I wouldn't be doing this if I thought it would be dangerous. Trust me." He leaned toward me, kissing me ever so gently.

How was I supposed to say no after that?

With no other choice, I followed him onto the dock.

It swayed underneath my feet, already making me a bit apprehensive. At the end of the dock was a tiny building that we used to change into our bathing suits.

Then, once our life jackets were secured, we jumped onto the jet ski.

"Are you okay?" Drew asked, looking back at me. "Just remember, hold on tight."

"Well, I would be a lot better if I wasn't on this thing."

"Oh, come on, it's not that bad. Live a little."

"That's exactly what I want to do – live."

"I'm not going to kill you."

"Yeah, but the ocean might."

"Stop worrying and just try to enjoy yourself, alright?"

I sighed. "Fine." I held on tightly to the straps on his jacket knowing that if I didn't I would go flying as soon as he jumped a wave.

He turned on the engine. It purred like a kitten, sending vibrations through my body. Somehow, they made it easier to relax.

I leaned into him as soon as we started our trek toward the open water.

To my amazement, it was, in fact, quite calm. It looked like a sheet of steel had been placed on the Earth.

"Wow..." I whispered. "This is beautiful."

"Isn't it?" He agreed, leaving the jet ski in an idle position so we could just enjoy ourselves. "I told you."

"No need to rub it in."

"Well, you should just start listening to me more often."

"I listen to you all the time. You're my agent, remember?"

"But, more importantly, I'm your husband." He turned around to kiss me, lips lingering on mine. It was a little awkward given the bulk of our life jackets, but I still savored every second of it, addicted to this man.

He ran his fingers through my hair before turning around and flooring the gas.

We went flying, cutting through the water like butter.

And, I must admit, that at the end of the night, I was enjoying myself. With the adrenaline running through my veins, I felt a high like never before.

I felt like I was on the top of the world, reigning supreme with my faithful king by my side.

Life was perfect.

*****

Don't miss out!

Visit the website below and you can sign up to receive emails whenever Van Cole publishes a new book. There's no charge and no obligation.

https://books2read.com/r/B-A-RTRV-JGFHC

BOOKS 2 READ

Connecting independent readers to independent writers.

Also by Van Cole

3 Man Huddle: MMM Best Friend Romance
His Alpha Wolf: Gay First Time Romance
A Dragon's Miracle: Gay Dragon MPREG Romance
Double-Teamed: MMM First Time Football Romance
His Football Star: Gay Second Chance Romance
Love In My Town: MM First Time Romance
Training A Hockey Star
Game Night
Double Shift
Take A Shot
Dear Professor
Getting Inked
Ninth Inning
Triple Threat
Seducing My Best Friend's Brother
My Protector
The Blueprint
Show Me The Way
End Zone
Matched To His Tiger
Love At First Puck
My Straight Boss
Falling For The Alpha
My Boss
On Thin Ice